# HAVE YOU HEARD ABOUT EPIC! YET?

We're the largest digital library for kids, used by millions in homes and schools around the world. We love stories so much that we're now creating our own!

With the help of some of the best writers and illustrators in the world, we create the wildest adventures we can think of. Like a mermaid and narwhal who solve mysteries. Or a pet made out of slime.

We hope you have as much fun reading our books as we had making them!

epic! originals

# DIARY OF A 5TH GRADE
# OUTLAW

## GINA LOVELESS

### ILLUSTRATIONS BY
### ANDREA BELL

Andrews McMeel
PUBLISHING®

# NOTE:

**I**f you are reading this diary, you need to know 5 things:

1. Mom and Dad gave me this as a back to school gift. It took me a month to start writing, but here I go!

2. You're about to learn a ton of cool basketball moves. Basketball is the best sport ever, and I've been playing it since second

grade. I love it more than double chocolate fudge ice cream. Yeah, that much.

3. I miss my best friend, Mary Ann, but nothing will stop me from winning her back.

4. Mom, I know this is you. Please stop reading.

5. Mom, since you're probably still reading, could you pick up double chocolate fudge ice cream at the store?

## MONDAY, OCTOBER 3

I need the first thing I write in this journal to be about something that happened today that first made me feel as good as red velvet cake but then ended up making me feel like mud caked on my shoe.

See, I was at recess, walking by the basketball court, when I heard this boy say, "You guys don't get it. I'm without a doubt the best basketball player at our school. I can beat anybody anytime at any shot."

I stopped short. I folded my arms and couldn't help but stare at the kid. When the boy looked at me, his face turned the color of marinara sauce. "What are you looking at?" he said.

"It's just that . . ." I walked over to the court and flipped my hair. "How do you know you're the best basketball player at

Nottingham Elementary if you haven't played everyone?"

The two boys next to Marinara looked at me like my hair was made of pasta. One kid was tall and skinny like a breadstick. The other looked like a ravioli.

I wondered if they were still hungry from lunch like me.

"Who is she?" asked Marinara, jabbing a thumb at me.

"I have no idea," said Ravioli.

"I think she's in Ms. Gaffey's class," said Breadstick.

"I'm Robin Loxley," I said. "And I challenge you to a basketball duel."

Marinara shrugged his shoulders. "Never heard of you, but I'll beat you at any shot."

I pointed to the three-point line. "First shot is from there, with one hand behind your back, standing on one foot, and one eye closed."

"No way," said Ravioli.

"That's impossible," said Breadstick.

"You're on," said Marinara.

I stepped up to the half circle painted on the blacktop and put my hood up. "I'll go first."

Marinara passed me the ball. It was showtime. I nailed the shot just like this:

It was a pretty cool shot. But they didn't seem to think so. None of the boys went "Woot-woot!" or "Yowza!" or other noises cartoon characters make.

Marinara walked up to my spot, and I got out of his way. Breadstick passed him the ball. Marinara dribbled it a couple of times. He passed it through his legs. Then he put his left hand behind his back, closed his right eye, stood on one foot, and stuck his tongue out. Right at me. He launched the ball into the air like a catapult.

I held my breath while it went like this:

I waited again for the other kids to rush over and put me on their shoulders. I waited for Marinara to come over and say, "I'm so sorry, Basketball Goddess. You are the queen of these courts!" I waited to even get a high-five or a fist bump.

But . . . Yeah. That didn't happen.

"You cheated!" yelled Marinara. "I don't know how, but you cheated."

Now if he'd said, "Whatever, I'm bad at losing, and I don't wanna see your face anymore," at least that would have been honest. I would have just walked away.

But . . . Yeah. That *definitely* didn't happen.

Because nobody calls me a cheater.

"You saw me throw the ball, and it went in," I said. I walked over to the grass and picked up the basketball. "Take it back!" I said.

"No! And give us our ball!" Marinara yelled.

Okay, before I draw what happens next, I want to also write that I didn't mean for it to go down the way it did. Sometimes I get a little fired up when something isn't fair. I knew the *right* thing to do was take a long breath and walk away.

But . . . Yeah. You guessed it. The right thing didn't happen.

# CHAPTER 2

**N**ow Marinara's face wasn't red from being angry. It was red because I made his nose bleed.

"AGHH!" he yelled.

I pulled back my hood. I felt horrible. "Hey, I am really sorry," I said. I may have been mad, but I didn't mean to hurt the kid.

"Aaron! You okay, dude?" asked Breadstick.

Aaron wiped his tears with his hands. Then he used his sleeve to clean the blood from his nose.

"I'm fine," he said.

"I didn't mean to—" I started to say.

Then all three of them turned and stared at me with eyes that said, "Get off our court now!"

"GET OFF OUR COURT NOW!" yelled Aaron.

At first my feet just wouldn't move. But when Aaron headed toward me, I found my legs and made my way back to the school.

"I better never see you on this court again or there'll be trouble!" said Aaron.

My walk of shame led me across the playground and past the jungle gym. Well, I tried to walk past it, but there was a swirly line of kids in the way, waiting to climb up the steps. At the top was Nadia. She's a girl in my class who likes to boss around any kid who will let her.

Nadia saw me from the top of the jungle gym. "Hey! No line jumpers, Robin," she said. "I'll charge you six times the price if you try to cut to the front."

She was talking about the Playground Tax. If you want to do just about anything fun during recess, you'd better cough up your Bonus Bucks to Nadia or one of her minions. Or else.

Bonus Bucks are this thing Principal Roberta came up with. When you do something really

good in class, like ace a quiz, use good manners, or help another kid with something, you get awarded Bonus Bucks.

Principal Roberta has all kinds of awesome prizes in her office that you can spend your bucks on, like 10 extra minutes of recess, getting to wear pajamas for the day, or— my personal favorite—a pass to get out of homework for a whole week!

Nadia isn't great with manners, and helping others is like a foreign language to her. Instead, she gets her Bonus Bucks from other kids. She and the other mean kids who work for her rotate at different stations all over the playground, making kids pay up Bonus Bucks to have any fun.

Want to play four square? Hand over three bucks. Want chalk to play tic-tac-toe on the blacktop? Better have one Bonus Buck for each color chalk you want. Stuff like that.

Nadia gets the big bucks by collecting them at the top of the jungle gym. She charges five whole Bonus Bucks for that.

I know . . . I know . . . It's pretty crazy. The worst part is that Nadia can't even spend the bucks because it would give her away to the teachers and Principal Roberta. She just likes ruining everyone else's fun. The teachers don't have a clue about what is going on, because kids still spend some of their bucks on rewards. Plus, kids are afraid to tell the teachers. Not just because of what Nadia might do, but because they are worried that if anyone finds out, Principal Roberta will end it all, and the Bonus Bucks will be taken away forever. So kids pay Nadia their Playground Tax and go on earning more bucks.

Unlike a lot of the other kids at my school, I'm not so easily pushed around by Nadia.

And I wasn't even trying to get onto the jungle gym—I was trying to get past it. I wormed my way through the line. When I got to the other side, someone tapped me on the shoulder and said, "Hey!" in an annoyed voice.

The hair on the back of my neck stood up. Was Aaron looking to get even?

I pulled my hood over my head and spun around on my heels with my fists up. If I had to defend myself, I was ready.

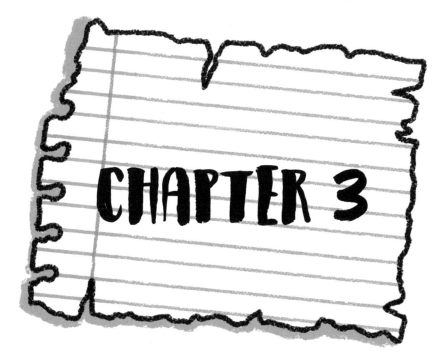

# CHAPTER 3

It was a good thing I looked before I swung, because the person who grabbed my shoulder wasn't Aaron. It was this girl, Jenny. She stared at me like I was made of Jell-O and she was trying to figure out what flavor I was.

My stomach growled. I really needed to pack bigger lunches.

"Here," Jenny said, handing me an envelope. "It's for Mary Ann's birthday. She says sorry it's so last minute, but her mom just said it was okay to have it."

"Oh . . . ," I said, dropping my fisticuffs.

I opened the invitation. It was so pretty.

As a rule, I am not a big fan of parties. I get shy around lots of people and usually just hide inside my hoodie. And they always serve pizza, which is one of my least favorite foods. Plus, my parents don't have a whole lot of money, so I can never buy presents as nice as other kids can.

But this time, none of those things mattered. The name on the invitation made this the one party I wanted to go to: Mary Ann Cassidy.

I met Mary Ann in kindergarten. On the first day, nobody had talked to me all morning, and then she came over and asked if she could use my crayons. I thought Mary Ann was going to walk away with them. But she sat down next to me and colored her picture of a pig and talked to me about why she thought pigs were gross because they're always covered in dirt and she hates getting dirty. I laughed and laughed.

We were best friends ever since.
Thick as thieves.

Well . . . until the Saturday
before school started. That's when
everything changed.

Mary Ann had a big ballet recital. She'd been practicing all summer long, and she invited me to come see it. But the morning of the recital, my mom picked up a work shift at the restaurant, so I didn't have a ride. My dad gets something called seizures, so he can't drive.

Dad tried to call Mary Ann's mom to see if she could pick me up, but nobody answered. He left a message for her mom to call him back, but she never did.

Then the school year started, and we weren't in the same class. I tried to find her at recess, but she was hanging out with Jenny.

I waved to her, but she didn't wave back. So I just left her alone. It has been weird ever since.

But if she invited me to her party, then I still had a chance at being her friend! Maybe I could talk to her and tell her what happened. And maybe we could even be *best friends* again. Now I just had to figure out a really, really good gift.

After the recess bell went off and we all headed back to class, there was a *tap-tap-tap* on the intercom.

"Hello, Nottingham Elementary! This is Principal Roberta. As some of you may know, I'm leaving in just a few short hours to attend a conference for the rest of the week. Assistant Principal Johnson will be in charge while I am gone. But don't worry, you will still be able to earn your Bonus Bucks, so keep up that positive behavior! Have a great week, and I'll see you all on Monday."

Principal Roberta's big announcement reminded me to count my Bonus Bucks. I pulled them out of my desk and shuffled through the pile. 197. Sweet!

I was proud of myself for having as many bucks as I did. I only get okay grades, so most of my bucks came from doing classroom chores or being quiet when the rest of the class got noisy. Plus, I never paid Nadia's Playground Tax, I'd held onto a lot my bucks from last year, and I hadn't spent a single buck this year. I was saving up for something special.

At the end of the day before getting on the bus, I stopped by the principal's office to check out what prizes were still around.

Principal Roberta keeps the really big prizes on a bulletin board decorated to look like a treasure chest so kids could see what their options are.

That's when I saw it. The best-ever birthday present for Mary Ann.

200 BONUS BUCKS

PRINCIPAL

FOR THE DAY!

Stuck on the board between "Read Morning Announcements" and "Extra Pudding" was the coveted "Principal for the Day" badge.

Mary Ann always talked about what it would be like if she could rule the school. How there would be no tests, and recess would be twice as long. Now she could do it!

Well, for a day. But still!

It cost 200 Bonus Bucks. I was so close to having enough. All I had to do was earn three bucks between now and Friday, and I'd have the perfect present for Mary Ann's party.

Easy peasy, right?

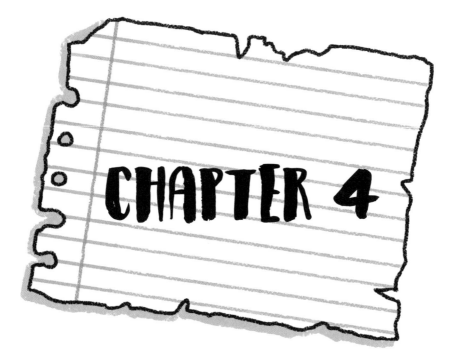

# CHAPTER 4

## TUESDAY, OCTOBER 4

Today started out like most days. During morning announcements, the twins in my class, Allana and Dale, rapped the school news. Allana always starts and then Dale raps the next line.

Principal Roberta left the school
    She went somewhere fun
We hear she's in Hawaii
    We bet she'll enjoy the sun
They say it's just this week
    They say it's for four days
But if we left for Hawaii?
    Ya know we'd try to stay!

Everyone cheered. Allana and Dale were no Savage Saucers, the best band on the planet, but they were my next favorite.

Then Ms. Gaffey made everyone settle down while she took attendance. Sammy, who was the smallest boy in fifth grade, asked if he could use the bathroom pass. But when he got out of his seat, he tripped and fell.

Nadia pointed at him and laughed. "Sammy, Sammy, what a whammy!"

Everybody laughed. Well, I didn't laugh. And Joan didn't laugh either. She sits behind me.

Before I had a chance to help, Joan was out of her seat and offering Sammy a hand. She hauled him up like he weighed as little as a cookie.

Even in my first class I was thinking about food! Maybe I needed a bigger breakfast . . .

Anyway, Joan rescued Sammy in half the time that most would because she's the tallest girl in fifth grade by like a foot. Or maybe even by a foot and a half.

Over the summer, Mary Ann and I came up with three possible reasons for why Joan is so tall:

Mom said it's because Joan is already going through "puberty." But I like our theories a little better.

Anyway, Joan returned to her seat, and Sammy made it to the bathroom and back without tripping again.

"Joan, that was very kind of you," said Ms. Gaffey. She walked over to Joan and gave her three Bonus Bucks. Then she turned to face the other side of the room. "Nadia. How about you follow Joan's example and be helpful? Come hand out today's math quiz."

Nadia scrunched up her face. She walked like a slug to the front of the class, grabbed the stack of papers from Ms. Gaffey's hand, and moved up and down the rows slapping a quiz on each desk.

When she got to Joan, she slammed the paper down with an extra *WHACK!*

"That's quite enough, Nadia," said Ms. Gaffey. "Unless you prefer to take your quiz during detention."

Things settled down after that. Ms. Gaffey asked us to raise our hands when we were done with our quizzes. Then she collected the paper and handed back the last quiz.

After trying my hardest to solve all of the multiplication problems on the page, I raised my hand. Ms. Gaffey came over and handed me my last quiz.

I closed my eyes before seeing the grade, then placed the paper facedown on my desk. I'm not the best at math, so whenever I get an assignment back, my routine is to flip the paper over while squinting with my right eye to see what I got. Kind of like ripping off a bandage so it hurts less.

I opened my right eyelid just enough to see the top of my paper.

I got an A!

I immediately opened both eyes to make sure I wasn't imagining things. Sure enough, there it was. A big letter "A" at the top of my sheet. Then I saw the thing that made me *really* excited. There were two Bonus Bucks attached at the top with a paper clip.

"Nice job, Robin," Ms. Gaffey said. "You're really improving."

Getting better at math was great and all, but all I could focus on was getting two more Bonus Bucks. I didn't need multiplication to figure out my total. I was at 199. Just one more buck and victory would be mine! Well, it would be for Mary Ann. She was going to freak out when I gave her my gift.

My day got even better in gym class when Coach Theckler said it was a free day. That means we can use whatever equipment we want. When somebody tells me I can do whatever I want, there is only one thing I want to do.

I ran straight for the basketballs. There were only two left in the equipment bag, so I grabbed the first one I could get my hands on.

I started dribbling toward an open hoop, but the ball didn't have much bounce. When I turned around to switch it out for the last ball, that ball was gone. I looked around the gymnasium and saw

Joan dribbling with the other ball on the opposite side of the court.

It would take way too long for Coach Theckler to put air in the flat basketball. The last time I asked him, he forgot where he'd put the pump, and I ended up searching through a dark, dusty closet for most of class instead of shooting hoops.

I walked over to Joan and tapped her on the shoulder. Well, she's really tall. It was more like I tapped her on the middle of her back.

She turned around sharply and looked down at me.

"What?" she asked.

"Can we share the basketball? The other one's kinda flat."

"No, thanks," Joan said.

I stopped, surprised. I hadn't expected for Joan to be so cold. She had been so nice to Sammy in math class. I tapped her on her back again.

"What?" she asked again. This time she didn't turn around.

I walked around to the front of her. "Can you *please* share the basketball with me?"

"I don't have time to run around the court chasing down your missed shots," said Joan. "I'm practicing to make the travel team."

The travel team plays basketball against kids from all over the county, not just our school district. There are only a few spots on the team so they only take the best of the best. I want to play for it, too, but Mom is always working night shifts at her job, so she can't drop me off. Since Dad only takes the bus, and there aren't any bus stops near where they practice, I can't make it to tryouts or practices.

My nose crinkled up like I smelled something rotten. It wasn't fair for Joan to hog the last good basketball because she thought I was a bad player. I grabbed the ball out of her hands, swiveled my hips toward the net, and fired at the hoop. It swished straight through.

"What missed shots?" I said.

Joan got the ball and dribbled it back to me. Without even bending her legs, she shot the ball over my head, and it went right through the net, too.

"That's an easy shot," Joan said.

My grin disappeared.

"True," I said. I mean it wasn't *that* easy. But that was totally not the point. "I was going easy on you to test your skills."

Joan laughed. "Who are you?"

"Aww, come on," I said. "I sit right in front of you. You know who I am."

Joan shrugged. "I don't really pay attention to other kids. They mostly spread dumb rumors about why I'm so tall. Can you believe someone was telling kids that I worked out using a taffy machine?"

*Cross that one off my list.*

My face felt warm. I pulled my hood up over my head. "Look, we both want to play," I said, as I walked over and grabbed the basketball. "So how about we do just that. First one to miss a shot loses the ball."

"Fine," said Joan. "Whatever gets you off the court faster."

I thought getting the ball would be quick. But dang, Joan was good at basketball. Like, really good. I started to wonder if this game would ever end.

Coach Theckler blew his whistle. "Two-minute warning," he said. "That's two minutes."

Okay, so it would clearly end in two minutes.

Suddenly, tall-as-an-oak-tree Joan didn't seem so tall and strange. She was a beast at basketball, and that was really cool.

"Why are you staring at me?" Joan asked.

"You're just awesome at playing ball," I said.

"Oh," Joan said, and blushed. "Thanks. You're pretty good, too."

For a few seconds we just stood there not saying anything.

"One minute!" Coach Theckler yelled.

"Hey, Joan," I said. "Would you like to eat lunch together?"

Joan smiled. "Sure. And you can call me LJ," she said. "That's the nickname my family gave me. It's short for Little Joan."

*Little* Joan?" I laughed so hard my hood fell off of my head. "But you're the tallest kid I know!"

"At my house," she said, "I have two brothers and two sisters, and they're all taller than I am."

"Okay then. LJ it is."

"And then maybe we can play basketball at recess," LJ said.

"Yes!" I said. "The two best basketball players should definitely play together."

"Two best . . . ," she said. Then LJ lifted her right hand and flung the ball at the hoop. It slid right through again. She looked back at me and winked. "But one clear winner."

# CHAPTER 5

**LJ** and I did hang out at recess. We were going to play basketball, but Nadia's goons were stationed at the courts.

LJ didn't have any bucks with her, and I couldn't spend any because of Mary Ann's present.

Then I had a pretty great idea.

"Want to go chill by the school wall?" I asked.

Okay, not the greatest idea. But at least we weren't just wandering around looking like two lost puppies.

As we leaned back against the brick, I had a clear view of the monkey bars and watched kids climbing to the top of them. But before most of them could even start swinging around, Nadia was sending them down the way they came up.

"I wonder what's going on," I said.

"You didn't hear?" asked LJ. "Nadia is making everyone pay a triple tax this week."

"What? Why?"

She shrugged again. "Maybe she just feels like being triple mean."

A triple tax was insane. The regular tax was already ridiculous. Who would pay three times as much to do something they *should* be able to do for free?

"But that's not fair. Kids can't earn bucks fast enough to keep up with that," I said.

LJ nodded. I threw my hood up over my head. Even though

I never paid Nadia's tax and even though I was definitely not going to pay her triple tax, what she was doing really made me upset. It was wrong.

"We need to do something about it."

LJ stopped nodding.

"I don't know . . . ," she said.

"Come on," I said. "Let's put our heads together and think."

The only thing that popped in my head was the basketball that bounced and hit Aaron's nose yesterday.

"We could talk to her," Joan said.

"Do you think that'll work?" I asked.

"My mom always says, 'Communication fixes everything, even a hole in a wall.'" She looked at the ground. "But my mom hasn't met Nadia."

"I don't know. . . ," I said. "I guess we can try." Then we both stood up and walked over toward the monkey bars. "What are you going to say?" I asked.

LJ said, "Oh . . . I was thinking that you could talk to her."

"Don't you want to do it? It's your idea."

"Well . . . yeah. But I'm not that good at talking."

I shook my head. LJ really was something else.

We got to the bottom of the monkey bars. I looked up. Nadia seemed really far away. Like I had to climb all the way to the clouds to reach her.

"Alright, let's go," I said.

"Well . . . ," LJ said. "How about I stay down here. For support."

I shook my head again. "Are you sure?" I asked.

LJ shrugged and looked at the ground.

I pulled on the strings of my hoodie and made my way up.

I thought about what I would say to Nadia.

Should I play it cool?

"Hey, Nadia. What's up? Wanna be a pal and lower that tax?"

Or should I play hardball?

"Listen here, Nadia. End the tax or there will be consequences!"

Maybe I could do something in the middle.

"Nadia, it would be great if you could get rid of the playground tax."

I thought about my options as I put my hands on the monkey bars and began to climb. But all the ideas I had left my head as soon as I got to the top.

"I want you to lower the tax," I said.

Nadia just stared at me.

"You don't even pay my tax."

"That doesn't matter," I said. "It's not okay. I'm not asking you to get rid of it altogether, just be a little fairer and bring it back to your normal amount. Can you do that?"

Nadia nodded her head up and down.

I looked down at LJ. Even though it looked like she was hundreds of feet below me, I saw her stick up both thumbs.

Then Nadia smiled. It worked!

Or so I thought.

"No," she said.

"No? Why not?"

"Cuz I don't negotiate with show-offs! It's a no. Now if you're not gonna pass over 15 Bonus Bucks, then get off the monkey bars, or everyone'll get even more taxing! NEXT!"

I felt my whole body get warm. I pulled even tighter on the strings of my hood. The hood squeezed my head just like all my feelings squeezed inside me.

"NEXT!" Nadia yelled again.

I slowly made my way down the monkey bars. With each step, I put together an idea.

"For the record," LJ said, "from what I could hear, that was awesome communicating on your part."

"Well, that's great, but I'm done talking," I said. "It's time to do something that's gonna work."

"Yeah, but what else can we do?" LJ asked.

"I know . . . ," I said. "I know just what we can do."

I whispered the plan to LJ, who smiled and said, "Oh . . . Oh boy!"

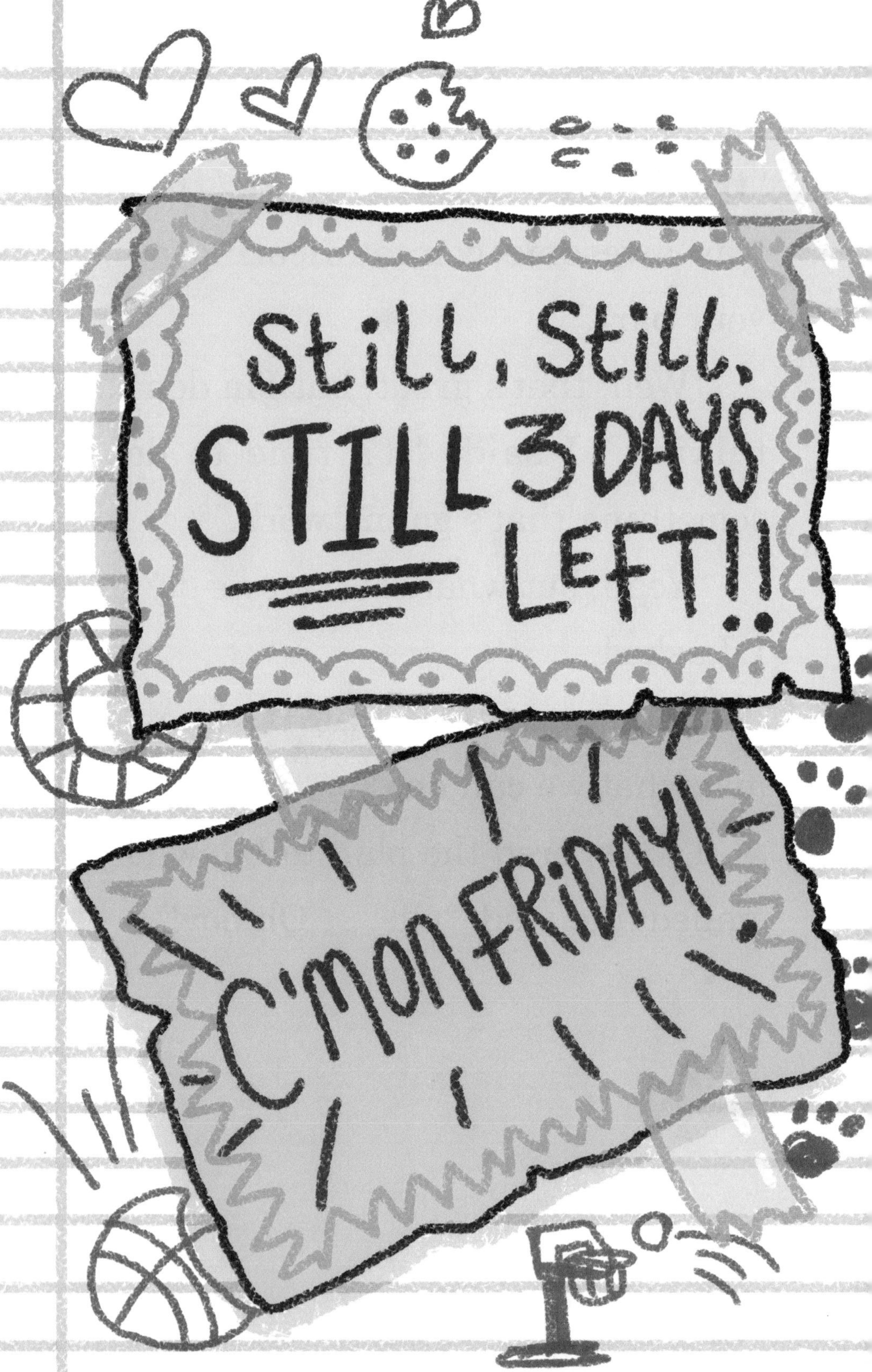
Still, Still,
STILL 3 DAYS LEFT!!
C'mon FRiDAY!

# CHAPTER 6

**LJ** and I were in the bathroom, sitting on the floor, waiting. I'd been writing notes all afternoon in class and was writing the last of them, which was an important part of the plan.

The speaker above our heads crackled. "Last call for buses. This is the last call for buses."

I put my backpack in the corner of the stall and turned to LJ. "Ready?" I asked.

LJ nodded. "Ready."

We snuck out into the hallway and began our trek.

Once we'd landed at Ms. Gaffey's classroom, we both knelt down in front of the door.

LJ popped up and down like a whack-a-mole.

"Coast is clear," she said.

We both ran to Nadia's desk first. When we opened it, I swear it glowed like gold. Nadia had so many Bonus Bucks in her desk, I couldn't even see any schoolbooks.

A loud creaking noise made LJ and me jump and turn from side to side, but nothing was there.

"We gotta move," I said.

"So, the plan is to give back all of the bucks to the other kids.

But there are so many. How many do we give to each kid?" LJ asked.

"No idea. Just throw a handful into each desk. It's better than nothing."

LJ nodded and grabbed the piles of bucks. There were so many, she had to stuff them in all her pockets, and I had to put some in my front hoodie pocket, too. LJ mumbled, "Wish we'd brought our backpacks."

As LJ dropped around 10 bucks in each desk, I followed and placed one of my notes on top. When we were finished, they looked like this:

"The 5th grade outlaw?" LJ asked.

"There wasn't time for me to write Best Basketball Player at Nottingham."

"True," she said. "Plus, then everyone would know it was me."

I laughed. "Anyway," I said, "let's move!"

Once we finished Ms. Gaffey's room, we sneaked our way into every single classroom, dropping bucks and notes as we went.

Nadia had so many bucks, we made it all the way to the kindergarten classroom before we ran out. When the last buck went into the last desk, I got this really warm feeling, like when I help Dad with the laundry. Which is not just because the laundry comes out as warm as a cup of hot chocolate.

Ooooh. With marshmallows on top.

*Note to self: Ask Dad for hot chocolate after writing this diary entry.*

Anyway, I looked at LJ. She looked like she felt as happy as I was.

It was a job well done for a couple of outlaws.

## CHAPTER 7

**WEDNESDAY, OCTOBER 5**

When I walked into Ms. Gaffey's room, every kid had bucks in their hands and was smiling. That warm feeling came back again.

And I also realized I never asked Dad for hot chocolate.

Allana and Dale tapped each other when I passed them and said,

*Our bucks are back*
*And with a note, too!*
*Does Nadia know?*
*Who cares? Wahoo!*
*Thank you to*
*The 5th Grade Outlaw!*
*Everyone cheer:*
*Hooray! Hoorah!*

Everyone clapped. I felt my cheeks go pink. I looked at LJ, and her cheeks were so red I thought they were on fire.

The room quickly went quiet. I looked to the door and saw exactly why.

Nadia had walked in. Everyone shoved their notes and bucks in their desks. But she didn't seem to notice. The next few seconds went like this:

Nadia walked over to her desk.

She put her backpack under her desk.

She placed her jacket on the back of her chair.

She opened her desk.

She looked down.

Her mouth opened.

And then . . .

Nobody raised their hand.

Nadia walked around from kid to kid and said, "Was it you? Was it you?"

Her eyes locked with mine.

*Bring it on*, I thought.

Nadia popped up in front of me and slammed her hands on my desk. "It was you, wasn't it?"

I didn't say anything.

"Yeah, I bet it was," Nadia says. "You'll pay for it. You were already gonna, now you *really* are."

I looked her straight in the eyes. I put my hood up.

"You're gonna get what's coming to you. You—" She looked me up and down. "Hoodser! Yeah. That's it! Because you've always got a stupid hoodie on and because you're a loser! Hoodser! Hoodser!"

Nadia was *not* gonna bully me. Not when I did the right thing. I stood up and was about to say something. But that's when Ms. Gaffey walked into the classroom and headed straight to her desk.

Nadia didn't waste any time.

"Ms. Gaffey, Robin stole my stuff."

"Is that true, Robin?" she asked.

"No, I didn't, ma'am," I said.

Okay, okay. I know it seemed like a lie. But the bucks weren't hers to begin with. And besides,

I didn't have any in my desk, so Nadia couldn't prove anything.

"She did!" Nadia whined.

Ms. Gaffey walked over to my desk. "Do you mind if I check your desk, Robin?"

I opened it up. "Go right ahead!"

Ms. Gaffey looked inside my desk. She moved my books around, but nothing came up! "Nadia, I don't see—"

But Ms. Gaffey stopped talking when she saw a piece of paper with the words *Nadia* and *Outlaw* flutter by her side.

Sammy's copy of my note had fallen to the floor!

# CHAPTER 8

I tried to pick up the note fast, but Ms. Gaffey got there faster. She looked at the paper with her lips pressed together really tight.

"Robin Loxley! To my desk, now!"

I squeezed the strings on the sides of my hoodie and walked up to the front desk.

"Is this your note?" she asked.

I didn't say anything.

"Fine," Ms. Gaffey said. "I've graded enough of your papers to know that's your handwriting. You called Nadia evil in this note. Even if there aren't items in your desk, this is teasing another student and passing notes in class. Go see Assistant Principal Johnson right now."

"What? But that's not fair!"

I looked at Nadia, and she stuck her tongue out at me. Ugh! She was the worst.

I looked at LJ next. She had turned a shade of red I'd only ever seen on Valentine's Day cards. But I shook my head at her. It was totally not her fault. I hoped she knew that.

On the way to see Mr. Johnson, I thought about what Ms. Gaffey just told me. I was sure that Mr. Johnson was going to give me Friday afternoon detention. I'd seen Nadia get sent to the principal's office enough times to know that if you did something that upset Ms. Gaffey and she was sending you there, you were going to get a detention.

This would be my first detention! Mom and Dad were not going to be happy about that.

But I also realized what *day* it would probably be. Friday! That would be during Mary Ann's party! How was I ever going to be best friends with Mary Ann again if I had to be in detention and couldn't make it to her party?

I walked into the office and looked for the assistant principal. He was standing by the counter with a look on his face like he'd just won a free pizza, and pizza was his favorite food.

"Ah, Robin, there you are." He lifted the counter and said, "Ms. Gaffey just e-mailed me. This way."

I passed behind the counter and followed him into his office.

I'd never really paid much attention to Mr. Johnson before. He looked like this:

"Now." He smiled even bigger and leaned back in his chair. "Just be honest with me so I can get to the bottom of exactly what happened."

I told him everything. I told him about Nadia and the tax. I told him about the triple tax. I told him about trying to talk to her and returning the bucks to the kids.

I left LJ out of it, so I guess I told him *almost everything*. But I didn't lie to him. I figured then Nadia would get in trouble and not me. I could go to Mary Ann's party. It was win-win.

"Thank you for explaining all of this to me," he said, and leaned back in his chair. "That makes this very simple."

I felt all the tough feelings leave my body. Mary Ann would be my best friend again! Nadia would get detention instead of me. It would all be better.

But. Yeah. Wowzer. That really didn't happen.

Mr. Johnson stood up.

"You're getting a Friday afternoon detention."

My heart sank. "W-What?" I stuttered. "But what about Nadia?"

"That's a good point," he said, and rubbed his chin. "But not just Nadia. It's the whole school."

I almost don't want to write down what happened next. It was so awful.

He leaned back in his chair again. This time, when I looked at his smile, I realized it didn't look friendly. It looked sinister. Like he won a free pizza and gave it to me even though he knew I hated pizza.

Then he said, "I'm suspending the Bonus Bucks."

# CHAPTER 9

"**I**'m sorry. Can you repeat that?"
I asked.

The shock of what Mr. Johnson
had said hit me just like the
basketball accidentally hit Aaron
on Monday—right in the nose!

But the words themselves
went in one ear, swirled around

a little bit, and then went straight out the other.

"It has been clear to me that the kids in this school are being rewarded way too much. And now, with all that you've just told me, that makes my decision simple. I'll get rid of the bucks for the rest of the week, and then I'll show that to Principal Roberta as evidence it's an unnecessary system."

*Oh no! Oh no no no!*

"No no no no," I said.

"I'll see you Friday afternoon for detention. You can return to class."

My head spun and my thoughts followed. Thoughts like:

What just happened?
Was that a dream?
Did I imagine that?
I must have, right?
What do I do now?
How do I fix this?
How many fixins did Dad put on my sandwich today?
And how am I still hungry even during a mess like this???

I walked out of Mr. Johnson's office and felt like I'd just done 100 push-ups and then 100 sit-ups and then ran 100 feet 100 times.

And then all the thoughts in my head started running like they were on fire and running fast was the only way to make the fire go out.

First, I thought, if the bucks were gone, how was I going to earn one more buck and give Mary Ann that gift? She would never forgive me or want to be friends with me again.

Then I thought, if the bucks were gone, why wasn't Nadia in

detention, too? Why was I the only one getting in trouble?

And last, I thought, if the bucks were gone, the whole school was going to hate me. There's no reason Mr. Johnson would tell anyone it was my fault. Right? Right. At least there was that small piece of good news.

My walk back to Ms. Gaffey's classroom felt like it took me forever.

On my way there, I heard the crackle of the speaker system.

"Attention, Nottingham Elementary," said Mr. Johnson. "It has come to my attention that the Bonus Bucks system has been heavily abused. Starting immediately, the Bonus Bucks and reward system will be suspended. That is all."

*Phew,* I thought. *At least he didn't say my name.*

# CHAPTER 10

**I** figured lunch would be equally bad. I walked over to a table in a corner to sit by myself and be as far away from everyone as possible.

I laid my head down on the table. Today couldn't possibly get any worse.

Then I heard a tray hit the table, and my head popped up.

But I didn't have to be worried at all. In fact, I smiled when I saw who had come over.

LJ pulled food out of her bag and said, "What did you say to the assistant principal?"

"I told him the truth about everything."

LJ and Sammy looked at one another. Allana and Dale did, too.

"Well, I think it's really cool what you did," said Sammy.

"I agree," said LJ. "You did what you had to do."

Allana and Dale rapped.

*You were really brave.*
  *Cuz Nadia's the worst*
*It's not your fault*
  *That the bucks plan burst.*

I pulled on the strings of my hoodie because I didn't want any of the other kids to see that my face was probably as pink as a fresh pack of bubble gum. I'd never had that many kids actually be nice to me at once.

I said, "Thanks."

"Hey, Hoodser," said a voice. I turned around, but I shouldn't have.

It was Aaron. He wasn't all that red-faced or bleeding anymore, but he did have a bandage over his nose.

Also, why did he call me Hoodser? That was the terrible new name Nadia had called me.

I turned back around and counted backward from 10. Maybe if I counted down all the way and didn't say anything, he would go away.

But yeah. That never seemed to work.

"I steal chip packs from the first graders," he said. "You should tell the assistant principal. Maybe he'll get rid of lunch!"

"Oh yeah," Sammy said. He stood up. "Maybe she will!"

That made Aaron laugh really hard. He walked away saying, "Whatever" and "What a loser" under his breath.

"You don't have to help," I said to the table. "It's my fault."

"No way," LJ said. "Not just your fault."

It was really nice of her to say that. I wondered if maybe she felt bad that everyone was being mean to me when she had helped, too. But I was definitely not telling anyone she was involved. It was my idea, and I'd take the heat for it.

"Yeah," Sammy said. "And you got us some of our bucks back!"

Allana and Dale nodded and rapped.

*You stood up for us*
  *When you didn't have to*
*Now we'll do*
  *The same for you!*

Now my cheeks felt so warm they must have been as pink as an uncooked pork chop. I pulled tighter on the strings of my hoodie. It was so tight around my face that the only thing the other kids could see was my eyes.

But they were definitely smiling.

When we all ran outside for recess, I walked toward a tree. I was going to say something to the group about hanging out next to it, but I saw Mary Ann was sitting underneath it with Jenny.

"I'll be right back," I told everyone.

But because my hood was so tight around my face, it came out like "Mmph ee frst blck."

Since I had Friday afternoon detention, I had to tell Mary Ann I couldn't make it to her party. I was going to do it just like when I looked at the grades on my quizzes. Just rip off the bandage. I loosened my hoodie so she'd be able to see my face.

When I got closer, I closed my eyes.

"Oh. Hey, Robin," Mary Ann said.

That was the moment just like when Ms. Gaffey put the paper down on the desk in front of me.

I opened my eyes, and the words came out of my mouth faster than anything ever has.

"I'm-really-sorry-but-I-can't-make-it-to-your-birthday-party-on-Friday-please-don't-be-mad-at-me-

I-am-so-sorry-you-have-no-idea-
I-don't-want-to-say-why-but-you-
have-no-idea-how-bad-I-feel."

She stared at me like I had just swallowed a thousand licorice sticks and she couldn't tell how they all fit in my stomach.

*Man, I could really go for a licorice stick while I write this.*

Anyway, back to the playground.

Mary Ann crossed her arms and shook her head. "You're not coming to my big day? Again?"

"I'm . . . I'm . . . ," I stuttered.

But Mary Ann cut me off. "Whatever. At least you told me this time."

My jaw dropped, and I turned around and walked back toward the kids from my class. It hurt too much to stay and see the look on her face.

My body felt warm, but it was because I was mad and sad at the same time, and it made my belly feel awful. There was only one reason I felt like this: Nadia.

Nadia was the reason my tummy hurt. Nadia was the reason I couldn't see my old best friend on Friday. And she was the reason Mary Ann was even being mean to me!

I looked up and found that Sammy, Allana, Dale, and LJ were all still in the same spot where I left them.

"Do you guys want to play four square?" Sammy asked.

"Did you read the note before Ms. Gaffey took it?" I asked. "Keep your bucks to yourself!"

"Yeah," Sammy said. "I guess I thought Nadia wasn't taking bucks anymore."

"Oh no," LJ said, "she is. Nadia is straight cold. Even though kids can't earn them back, she's still taking them."

I shook my head. All the mad feelings in my body took over the sad feelings. This was a new low even for Nadia.

"Nadia's gone off the tracks!"

Everyone nodded their heads.

Allana and Dale rapped their response.

*But what can we do*
  *You tried your best*
*And she didn't change*
  *It's all just a mess.*

"Then that's what we need to do for recess today!" I said. "We need to come up with a plan to stop Nadia. Who's with me?"

Sammy, LJ, Allana, and Dale all said, "ME!"

# CHAPTER 11

**THURSDAY, OCTOBER 6**

So, yesterday's recess didn't go so well. We thought about how we'd stop Nadia for a while, but nobody could think of anything.

Then LJ gave Frida, one of Nadia's minions, some of her bucks so we could play four square. Then we played four square until the bell rang. It wasn't great.

Okay, it wasn't just not great. It was next-level terrible.

Yeah, I had fun with my new friends. But we had to give Nadia bucks AND we still didn't have a plan for how to beat her.

Today, at lunch, LJ and I agreed we had to come up with a way to stop Nadia, no matter what.

The second our feet hit the playground, Sammy, Allana, and Dale ran over to us.

"She . . . She . . . She . . . ," Sammy said. He breathed really hard, like Uncle Peter does when he eats too much at Thanksgiving and then tries to chase my 2 year old cousin, Jones. "Sorry. I'm bad at running."

Allana and Dale nodded to each other.

*Nadia has taken*
   *A turn for the worse*
*She's still taxing kids*
   *Still filling up her purse*
*There's still a triple tax*
   *But the worst part of all*
*Is that nobody's got bucks*
   *And she still won't give*
   *out balls*

*Because they don't have bucks*
   *She's taking other stuff instead*
*Like snacks, pencils, and gum*
   *And someone even gave her*
   *their bed!*

We all looked at Dale.

"Well, nobody gave up their bed," he said and looked down at his feet. "'Instead' was just really hard to rhyme with."

It was time to take Nadia down once and for all. I put up my hood and I took a deep breath.

But all I got out was "We need to—" when Nadia yelled something from the top of the monkey bars:

I couldn't believe it.

As in I really, really could NOT believe it.

Would Nadia actually give up half her bucks? I didn't know, but it was the only chance I had.

If I won the tournament, I'd give everything I got to the kids. Nadia would be so angry, but there'd be nothing she could do.

Well . . . I'd give back everything except just one buck. That way, whenever Principal Roberta came back and heard all of Mr. Johnson's stuff about the bucks, maybe she would think to herself, "Nope, I think it works just fine." Then she would make an announcement: "The Bonus Bucks are back in action kids," and then I could get the Principal for the Day badge and still give it to Mary Ann.

I turned to the group. "Do you all know what this means?"

Everybody nodded.

"It's going to be a really boring recess tomorrow because basketball is super boring," Sammy said.

My hand went straight to my chest. His words kicked all the air out of me. "No," I said, barely.

LJ laughed. "I think I know," she said. "It means it's a chance for us to give some bucks back to the kids again."

I nodded my head.

"That's a great idea," said Allana.

"But who's going to compete?" asked Dale.

"Well, you happen to be looking at the two greatest basketball players at Nottingham Elementary School," I said.

"Who should we be looking at?" Sammy asked.

I sighed. "LJ and me," I said. "We're both awesome at basketball."

"One of us is slightly better than the other," LJ said, "but we don't talk about it."

Sammy, Allana, and Dale all gathered closer to me and LJ. They said things like "Wow" and "So cool" and things real friends say when they're excited for you.

I had real friends who believed me when I said I was one of the best basketball players.

Now, the really big thing was that I couldn't let them down.

# CHAPTER 12

**FRIDAY, OCTOBER 7**

So, I just realized that I never wrote anything yesterday about what happened other than recess. But that's because recess was such a big deal, I kinda forgot what else happened.

Well, it was just like that today. All the super big and crazy things that went on started at lunch. As we ate, all anybody could talk about was the basketball tournament.

Allana and Dale rapped about our chances of winning.

*There's two of you*
  *Playing today*
*And that Nadia?*
  *She's gonna pay!*
*She's gonna pay*
  *You half the tax*
*Cuz you're gonna win*
  *And get half her stack . . . s.*
  *Stacks. Yeah . . . stacks.*

Dale looked at Allana. "Can I be the one who starts the raps for a little while? I'm having a hard time rhyming stuff lately."

Allana said, "Sure," and ate her applesauce.

Sammy tried to be nice but had a hard time with it. "I'm sure you two will do a really good job even though basketball is such a yawn."

LJ and I looked at one another, rolled our eyes, and laughed.

"What do you think the tournament is going to look like?" LJ asked. She picked at the crust on her sandwich.

"I don't know," I said. And it was true. Last night, lying in bed, I'd come up with a worst-case scenario, and it had to do with the lake just down the street from the school:

The recess bell rang, and LJ and I walked outside. I hated to say it, but I was a little nervous. I didn't know what tricks Nadia had up her sleeve.

In the middle of the basketball court, Nadia stood with a long-sleeve shirt on. If she had any tricks, she was definitely hiding them up there!

LJ and I stood on the free-throw line while Nadia stood in the very center of the court. She had five basketballs by her feet. I wondered how she'd found so many, when Coach Theckler didn't even have more than two for gym.

Nearly every kid stood around the court watching to see what would happen or getting ready to be in the tournament. Everyone except Mary Ann and Jenny. They were sitting under the tree again, playing Miss Mary Mack. Mary Ann looked over and locked eyes with me, but then she turned back to Jenny.

I wasn't surprised. I didn't show up for her ballet recital, so why would she want to see me in this big tournament?

"Alright!" Nadia said. "Listen up. This competition will be two rounds. The first is Around the

World. Anyone who misses any shot is out of the competition. If there are too many kids once you make it around, you'll have to go back around the court again."

"How many is too many?" a boy asked.

Nadia ignored the boy and went on. "Second part is going to be one-on-one. First one to three points wins. Every basket is a point no matter where you shoot it from."

"And the winner really gets half your tax?" Sammy asked.

"That's what I said yesterday," Nadia snapped. "Now let's get this thing started."

LJ and I walked over to where the baseline and the lane lines met. "Do you think this seems too easy?" LJ asked.

"Nah," I said. "Around the World is hard for some people."

"I'm not one of those people," a boy said. LJ and I turned around to see who was talking.

This boy from the other 5th grade class, Ty Lisborn, stood behind LJ. I had seen Ty a few times on the playground before, but only from a distance. His face always had a scary scowl on it. He was the kind of kid you really didn't want to bother. Ty looked like this:

"I'm gonna beat you at every shot," he said.

I put my hood up. For whatever reason, this was the week of kids bragging about their basketball skills.

"We'll see about that," I said.

LJ patted me on the back. She leaned down and whispered in my ear, "One of us is gonna win. We've got this!"

By the end of the Around the World round, every kid was out. Every kid except LJ, Ty, and me.

And Ty was not a good sport about it. With every shot I made, he spat out an insult.

"Easy shot."

"Gonna miss the next one."

"Pfft. Lucky."

"Next one'll flop."

"Think you're special?"

"What. Ever."

"Lame."

"Oooh. Miss Hot Shot."

"You think you're soooo great."

"Ugh!"

"Nice shot, Hoodser."

That's the one that did it.

"What did you say to me?" I'd ignored Ty at every other shot, but by the 11th one, it was impossible.

Plus, why did he call me the same stupid name as Nadia? How did all these kids who aren't in Ms. Gaffey's class know Nadia's new mean nickname for me?

"You heard me," he said. "Now I get to play against both of you losers in one-on-one."

I jumped toward him, but LJ grabbed my arm.

"Stop," she said. "Don't let Nadia kick you out before we even get started."

I sighed loudly because I was so annoyed. I wanted to say, "I'd like to see her try!" I wanted to say, "I'll kick Nadia off this court!"

But . . . yeah, I didn't say any of those things.

I just pulled on the strings of

my hoodie and tightened my hood around my face.

LJ leaned down next to me again. "Besides," she said, "it's better that he plays one of us first. Then we can beat him and play each other. It's a win-win."

I smiled and looked at LJ. "That's true!" I said. I turned back to Ty. He stuck his tongue out at me. "I'll go first," I said.

"No, let me," LJ said. "The best basketball player should go first."

"I know," I said, "that's why I was going to—" But LJ didn't hear me because she was already halfway across the court.

A crowd of kids gathered around me. They yelled things like, "Holy moly, Joan!" and "Yippee, Joan!" Even though they were yelling things that cartoon characters yell and it was to LJ and not me, I was still really excited for her.

And anyway, LJ was really good at basketball. If there was anybody who could knock Ty out of the competition, it was her!

With all the kids cheering for LJ around me, I looked over to the other side of the court. That's when I realized all of the kids standing on the other side of the court were also acting like cartoon characters.

But they were like the villains.

"Beat Joan!" they yelled.

"You've got this, Ty!" they said.

"Destroy her!" they screamed.

*Destroy her?* That seemed like a bit much.

Nadia explained the rules again, and then, when LJ and Ty both said they understood, she threw the ball up in the air. That's when Ty pulled a totally illegal move.

LJ fell hard, and the ball flew across the court. Ty let go of LJ's shoe and ran after the ball.

I couldn't believe Ty pulled such a dirty move! I looked at Nadia, waiting for her to blow her whistle, but she didn't.

"That's a foul!" I yelled.

"Yeah, it is!" Sammy said.

I looked at him, surprised. He answered the question that was in my head without me even saying it. "My older sister plays," he said. "I get dragged to all of her games."

Even Allana and Dale broke their usual rap and screamed, "Foul play! Foul play!" over and over again.

But Nadia ignored us. Instead, she walked over to the other side of the court, the side that was saying, "Good call, Nadia!" and "Way to get her, Ty!"

While LJ was doubled over on the court, Ty dribbled the ball just under the hoop. He shot and got it in.

Nadia blew the whistle. "That's 1–0, Ty!"

I ran over to LJ. She still hadn't moved since Ty made her fall. "Are you okay?"

LJ nodded her head.

Nadia blew her whistle again. "Nobody on the court except the two people playing!" she yelled.

I stuck my tongue out at her. "If she's hurt, you're going to get in big trouble!" I yelled. Then I leaned down toward LJ. "Are you sure?" I asked.

"I'm just really embarrassed," she said. "Everybody just saw me fall." LJ turned just a little bit so she could see my face. "Ty's going to play dirty the whole game, isn't he? And Nadia doesn't care."

I looked at Ty. He dribbled the ball under the hoop. "Are we going to keep playing or what?" he yelled.

"Yeah," I said. "I think so."

Nadia blew her whistle again. "I said off the court, HOODSER.

Or you're outta here, and this is the last match!"

I backed off the court and yelled, "You've got this, LJ!"

The kids around me roared with support. "You're the best, Joan!"

"You can do it!"

Then Sammy added, "We love you, Joan!"

I looked over at him. He blushed so pink I thought he might pop. "I mean . . . We like you a lot, Joan!"

I screamed and yelled with all the other kids on my side while the game went on, but just as LJ and I were afraid of, Ty pulled dirty move after dirty move.

He grabbed the back of LJ's shirt and scored on her.

He threw the ball at her shoe during check and then ran around her and landed his last point.

Nadia blew the whistle. "That's game!" she yelled.

The side that Nadia stood on cheered. The side I was on booed.

LJ hobbled over to me and the group. "I'm sorry," she said. "I really tried."

I nodded my head. "I know you did," I said.

I looked over at Ty. He pointed to his own eyes and then back at me.

I was ready to kick this kid's butt. For LJ. For Sammy, Allana, Dale, Mary Ann, and all the other kids who were being crushed under Nadia's tyranny.

# CHAPTER 13

"**Y**ou're toast," Ty said.

I ignored his insult.

I also felt hungry for toast. With butter and maybe some strawberry jam.

But I shook my head and got back in the game.

Nadia whistled. "Let's get this over with."

Within seconds of Nadia blowing her whistle, Ty pulled his first dirty move of the match.

I clutched my chest, my eyes squinted shut from the pain.

I heard the ball hit the backboard and then swish through the hoop. Nadia blew her whistle and said, "1–0, Ty."

His dirty move took a lot out of me, but I had to bounce back quickly if I was going to win this.

I opened my eyes and walked back toward the foul line. Ty walked alongside me.

"You have no ch—" he started to say, but then he fell, face-first onto the blacktop.

"Cheat!" a voice yelled. "She tripped him."

"No, I didn't," I said.

A girl with red hair standing on

the mean side of the court pointed at me. "Yes, you did!"

I looked down and saw a shoelace sticking out from under my sneaker that led all the way to Ty's shoe.

Not again!

"Oh no," I said and offered my hand to Ty. "I'm sorry. That was a total accident."

Ty reached for my hand, and for a half second I thought he was going to take it. But then he pushed my hand away, stood up, and brushed himself off.

"Whatever," he said. "You're going down."

Nadia blew her whistle. "That's a point to Ty for messing with him."

"What?" I said. "I stepped on his shoelace by accident. And he elbowed me in the chest on purpose!"

Nadia looked me straight in the eyes and said, "I didn't see Ty do nothing."

I'd never been so mad in all my life. It was bad enough when a boy who couldn't play basketball called me a cheater. At least I knew I hadn't done anything wrong then.

But in this game, Ty was being nasty, cheated left and right, and now he had two points. What shot did I possibly have? LJ played clean, and Ty beat her easily.

I looked over at my friends, feeling the lowest I've ever felt.

But then something unexpected and kind of awesome happened.

Sammy told everyone to be quiet. That whole side of kids stopped making any noise at all. Then Dale and Allana started this chant.

*Robin's fair!*
*Robin's good!*
*Robin's gonna win!*
*She's Robin Hood!*

They sang it over and over again. Then everyone on that side of the court joined in.

They thought I was fair! And good!

And I guess I couldn't shake having a nickname with *hood* in it. I always wore a hoodie, so the nickname wasn't that bad. It was way better than Hoodser! Plus, these kids thought I was gonna win!

If my friends believed in me . . . if all those kids believed in me, then I *had* to believe in myself. I didn't have to play dirtier. I had to be like the chant—fair and good.

So when Ty threw the ball at me during the check, instead of it hitting my foot, like he tried to do, I jumped back. It bounced where my feet were supposed to be, and I caught it.

I took another big jump backward, toward the three-point line, and shot the ball.

Boom! It went straight in! Didn't even hit the backboard or rim.

For the next shot, I charged him right after the check, and it surprised him. Since he was caught off guard, I was able to steal the ball, pivot, and shoot it in.

Another swish and another point!

On one side of the court, the cheers grew louder, and the chant about me started again.

On the other side of the court, the boos were so loud I almost couldn't hear the chant.

The last point was the biggest of them all. It was 2 to 2, and whoever made the next shot would win.

After the check, I tried to steal the ball from Ty again, but he moved too fast. He jumped back and shot the ball at the hoop.

I watched the ball as it arched toward the hoop, and I decided to run toward the left side of the hoop just in case.

Sure enough . . .

SWISH!

I put my hood down and looked over to the cheering half of the court. LJ, Sammy, Allana, and Dale all ran toward me. Then the rest of the kids did, too. LJ picked me up and put me on her shoulders.

"Robin Hood! Robin Hood!" all the kids who came over to cheer me chanted.

"Could we try Basketball Goddess? Or maybe just Robin?" I asked over their cheering voices. "I like the nickname. I mean, it's okay. But Robin's just fine."

They ignored me. "Robin Hood! Robin Hood!"

LJ walked me over to Nadia. "Let's claim your prize and do even more good today!" she said.

While I was up on LJ's shoulders, I did a quick look around the court.

Had Mary Ann come over? Did she see my victory?

And then I saw her, out on the grass, still sitting and talking with Jenny.

Even though this moment felt so good, I couldn't help but feel a little hurt.

I was bummed she didn't see me beat Ty. But at least she'd eventually get to see the reward from it. Then I could tell her the crazy story of how I'd won the final buck that made it all possible.

Nadia was talking to Ty and somebody else I couldn't see even from up on LJ's shoulders. She did not look all that happy to have to give me half of her Bonus Bucks, but hey, a deal was a deal.

"So, where's my prize?" I asked.

Nadia screamed, "Are you kidding me?" Her face was as red as the pepperoni on pizza.

She stormed past us toward the field. It was full of mud puddles from the rain this morning, but either Nadia didn't notice or she didn't care. All of the kids from her side followed her.

She turned back to face the kids still on the blacktop. "THERE IS NO PRIZE! I'M NOT SHARING ANYTHING WITH YOU!"

## CHAPTER 14

**LJ** helped me jump down from her shoulders, which was a good thing because I would have fallen if I'd tried to get down myself.

All the remaining kids and I walked over into the mucky grass.

"I'm sorry. Can you repeat that?" I said for the second time this week.

I thought maybe if I asked her to repeat herself, she'd say, "I said come on over to my desk after recess and I'll give you your prize." Maybe she'd even say, "You won fair and square, so let's talk about those bucks."

But . . . yeah, nothing even close to that happened.

"NO! I won't repeat that!" Nadia yelled.

I'd just flipped my hood down, and it was time to put it back up again. "But you said—"

"I don't care what I said! This whole thing was supposed to be a trap. You hurt my cousin's nose on Monday, and I wanted revenge."

The kid behind Nadia walked to
the side of her and showed his face.
It was Aaron!

Nadia just kept screaming. "You were supposed to lose to Ty, and everyone would laugh at you, and you ruined it! YOU RUINED IT!"

Ever since Tuesday, when I became buddies with LJ and she told me all the terrible stuff Nadia had been doing, I'd worked as hard as I could to undo it all. And now it turned out that Nadia had been trying to make me mad ever since Monday. Ever since the accident with Aaron's face.

So . . . I'm gonna have to write that another thing happened this week that I'm not really proud of, but only so it makes a little bit of sense.

Nadia had just made me feel *the maddest I've ever felt*. I'd tried to do a good thing all week, and every day Nadia had screwed it up. And now she hadn't messed it up with just me, she'd messed it up for every kid who was going to get their bucks back. And because I wouldn't be able to take even one buck, she'd screwed up my chance of getting Mary Ann the perfect birthday gift and winning back my best friend.

All my mad feelings and my sad feelings jumbled together. I felt my whole body get warm, from my fingertips to the tip of my nose.

That's when I saw a bunch of mud splatter all over Nadia.

I whipped around to see where it came from, but everyone was staring straight ahead.

Then I got pelted with a big wet glop of dirt right in the center of my hoodie.

And then . . .

MUD FIGHT!

Chaos broke out as kids on both sides of the field, including me, flung mud at the people across from them. I was so mad and it felt good to move and throw things. Everyone else must have felt that way too, because the mud fight lasted a long time.

We kept going, even when we heard the recess aide, Ms. Harrison, say, "Oh dear! Kids, stop!" Even when our eyes and hair and mouths were caked with mud.

We threw every piece of dirt and grass we could until Assistant Principal Johnson yelled, "STOOOOOOPPPPPP!!!"

# CHAPTER 15

**E**verybody on the field had frozen in place. It was like we all hoped that if we didn't move, Mr. Johnson wouldn't be able to see us anymore.

But, yeah, I don't know why any of us would have thought *that* was going to happen.

Mr. Johnson looked around at the field. His eyes locked with mine. I felt my body get so hot, I thought I might have turned into a cayenne pepper. Then he looked to my left and right.

"The following 5th grade students will head to my office after school for detention: Nadia, Joan, Ty, Sammy, Aaron G., Allana, Theodore, Dale, and Ricardo. A call will be placed with your parents to notify them.

"If your name has not been called, you will receive a letter in your file, and I will be calling your parents or guardians.

"And everyone will turn in a one-page paper on Monday about why it was a terrible idea to join a mud fight during recess. Now, everyone inside! Vamos!"

Nadia and I looked at one another like if we looked at each other hard enough, the other person might pop like popcorn.

Man, even in my worst moments, my stomach just would not quit!

She ran toward the building.

Then LJ tapped me on the shoulder. "Sorry," I said. I looked around at Allana, Dale, and Sammy. "I'm sorry to all of you. I know I'm the reason all of this happened. I made Nadia angry before any of you even knew me. And then . . ."

Nobody said a word. I thought I knew what they were thinking. That they all hated me. They didn't want to be my friends anymore.

But it turned out they didn't think any of that.

"Nadia is the worst person I've ever met," LJ said. "And I have a big brother who gives me noogies all the time and calls me a pipsqueak. And he's in college!"

Sammy nodded his head. "And every one of those kids who thought she was okay for doing all that she did is an enemy of this playground!"

Dale and Allana started another rap.

*It's not your fault*

*It wasn't just you*

*We all stood up*

*For the truth*

*Nadia's a bully*

*She's just plain mean*

*And we'd all happily fight*

*For the Basketball Queen.*

My eyes widened to the size of apples. "Allana . . . did you just call me Basketball Queen?"

Allana smiled. "It rhymed with mean!" she said. "But yeah, you deserve it."

Even though I'd just gotten my friends in afternoon detention with me, that was the last thing on their minds.

Plus, I had an awesome new nickname!

Actually, that didn't even matter to me anymore. It felt way better having really great friends.

But as we walked into the school together, things went downhill quickly. Everyone else made it through the doorway.

Everyone, except me.

Mr. Johnson said, "You're skating on very thin ice."

I looked from side to side and tried to hide my smile. "But there's no ice on the playground, sir. If anything, I'm wrestling in some very thick mud."

Mr. Johnson looked at me with a look like someone had taken away all that free pizza he'd won.

"You're more than aware of what I mean. A student who has never been in trouble before gets in trouble twice in one week? And it just happens to be the week the principal is gone? I'm onto you, Robin. Since you're already serving detention after school, for today's actions, you'll be serving detention all next week."

My jaw dropped to the floor. "But it's Nadia's fault!"

"This is the second time you've blamed Nadia for your actions. I would think long and hard about why you blame others for your wrongdoings. And you'll have plenty of time to think of that in detention. But one more wrong move, and you'll serve in-school suspension. Do you understand me?"

I flipped up my hood and turned to walk away.

Mr. Johnson slipped around me and stood in front of me again.

"No hoods in school," he said. "And answer me, please."

I slowly put my hood down. My head felt weird. Like there were clouds where my brain used to be. I usually put it up when I wanted to block myself just a little bit from the people around me.

But now Mr. Johnson was staring at me, and my head was uncovered, and I felt so strange.

"Yes," I said.

"Yes what?" he asked.

I sighed. "Yes, I understand."

He turned around and walked straight into his office.

As soon as I couldn't see him

anymore, I put my hood back up and headed back to Ms. Gaffey's room. The whole way there, all I could think about was Nadia and how I was in this whole mess because of her. Mr. Johnson didn't know what he was talking about.

Yeah, the first time I got in trouble, it was partly my fault. I did steal and write something mean about Nadia. But I was just giving back to everyone what was really theirs. If she hadn't taken from them, it never would have happened!

But this time Nadia was supposed to give up an item, and I was trying to give it back, and

Nadia wouldn't, so Sammy yelled, "mud fight" because he wanted to defend me, and I didn't stop him. I joined in!

Okay. Okay, now that I'm writing it down, I can sort of see how some of this is my fault.

But still! Nadia was not in the right, and she shouldn't be able to just get one detention and that's it!

I passed by a classroom and saw Mary Ann inside. There was a long line of kids leading up to her desk. She looked really sad.

And then something worse than detention clicked in my head.

Not only did Nadia keep me from having enough bucks to get Mary Ann a gift, but now, because of all the trouble from the mud fight, I bet *nobody* was going to make it to her birthday party!

As I headed into class, I realized I wasn't going to be able to get all my friends out of detention and to Mary Ann's pool party. But there was still a way I could get that Principal for the Day badge. And I was going to have to skate on some real, real thin ice to get it.

Or wrestle in some really thick mud. Whatever. You get the point.

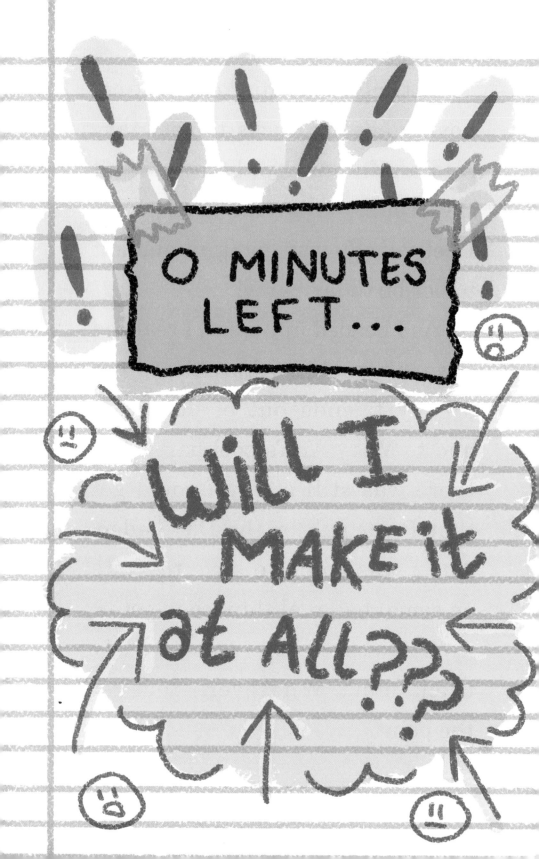

# CHAPTER 16

The whole rest of the afternoon, I'd kinda-sorta-not-really listened to Ms. Gaffey so I could figure out the rest of my plan.

At the end of the day, Ms. Gaffey told us we could do whatever we'd like at our desks as long as we stayed quiet. I turned around and waved my hand in front of LJ.

I leaned over her desk and whispered my idea to her. Then I pointed to Allana, who sat next to LJ.

LJ leaned across the aisle and tapped Allana on the shoulder. Allana turned, and LJ whispered the plan to Allana and pointed to Dale. And then Allana whispered the plan to Dale and pointed to Sammy. Finally, Dale whispered the plan to Sammy.

The end-of-the-day bell went off, and we all gathered at the back of the class. Sammy looked at me like

I had suddenly become an eggplant. "You're going to feel the badger?"

*Reminder for next time: Whisper down the alley is not the best way to start a plan.*

Nadia walked past us and gave me a mean look. I whispered as quietly as I could to Sammy so Nadia wouldn't hear any of it. "OHHHHHHHH," he said.

A squeaky squeal came through the loudspeaker. Mr. Johnson told us that everyone serving detention should wait in the back of the cafeteria while the bus crowd cleared out. We all headed there and did like he said.

Once everyone was gone, Mr. Johnson made us sit in two rows facing away from each other and at least five feet apart. Even though we were in the cafeteria, it felt a whole lot worse.

I felt a little nervous. But I knew time was ticking.

I turned around and raised my hand. "Excuse me, Mr. Johnson?"

Mr. Johnson turned and stared at me.

"Can I please use the bathroom?"

I swear, he didn't even move. "No bathroom breaks during detention."

"Seriously?"

"Seriously," he said, and turned around to walk down the aisle.

There went my plan! All in just a few seconds!

Well, that's what I thought at first.

But as I was turning around, I saw Sammy raise his left hand while holding his stomach with his right. He looked at me, winked, and said, "I don't feel so well."

Mr. Johnson stopped to look at Sammy. "I said no bathroom breaks during detention."

Then LJ looked at me and winked, too. "I don't feel so well either," she said.

"You heard what I just said Ms.—"

"But I think . . . I think I'm gonna . . ." Sammy ran toward the garbage can in the corner.

"Aww man . . . me, too!" LJ said, and ran past Mr. Johnson toward the garbage can.

"Why is this happening to me?" asked Mr. Johnson.

In that moment, I watched Mr. Johnson like a hawk. The second he turned to walk toward my friends fake hurling, I dashed out of the cafeteria for phase two of the plan.

# CHAPTER 17

I knew I didn't have a lot of time, so as soon as I shuffled my way to the hallway, I had to kick it into high gear!

After running around the corner and down the hall, I could see the door to the principal's office was open. I headed straight

to the bulletin board with all
the prizes.

But there went another part of
my plan. Every reward was gone!

Okay, it didn't have the evil laugh, but it felt like it did.

I quickly looked around the office to see where Mr. Johnson had hidden them, but I didn't see anything. Then I realized the prizes were probably in his office.

I turned the knob . . . but it was locked! I really should have thought of that.

Now I was really double stuck. Sneaking into the principal's office and stealing the Principal for the Day badge had been the entirety of phase two.

And then I heard the worst thing of all!

"Two kids vomiting . . . One hiding somewhere in the school . . . I tell you what . . ."

It was Mr. Johnson! If he caught me, that was it! In-school suspension had my name all over it.

I looked around the office to see if there was anything that could help. There was absolutely nothing that I could hide behind. I was about to give up, but then I saw the secretary's desk.

As fast but as quietly as I could, I jumped and rolled under the desk.

I stayed as quiet as I could.

Mr. Johnson walked right by me and unlocked his door. Then I heard a clicking sound coming from his office. "Hello, is this the parent or guardian of Joan—" He stopped and sighed under his breath. "Ma'am. Ma'am. Ma'am. I—Ma'am. If I could—"

Another click, this time louder.

"These parents will be the death of me."

Then there were a bunch of clicks again as he called Sammy's parents. That time he was able to say that Sammy had vomited and could be picked up early from detention.

But it was in the middle of that call that I felt an itch on my nose. I scrunched it around, but the itch stayed put. And then the itch got bigger and started going up my nose.

I was about to sneeze!

# CHAPTER 18

**S**crunched under the desk, I rubbed my nose with my finger as fast as I could and thought, *Please don't sneeze, please don't sneeze, please don't sneeze.*

Mr. Johnson put his laptop in a bag and as he walked toward the door, he said, "Tonight I start that painting tutorial."

I didn't know what a tutorial was, and I didn't have time to figure it out, because I was so busy rubbing my nose and thinking, *Just three more seconds, just two more seconds, just one more second!*

Then, I was pretty sure that two things happened at the exact same time.

**1**. Mr. Johnson closed the door to the main office.
**2**. My whole body sprung forward, and I went *ACHOO!*

I stayed very still. Even though I was like 99.9999999999999 percent sure that I sneezed at the same time the door closed, it was that 0.0000000000001 percent that made me sit in the same spot under the desk while I counted to 60 to make sure he was definitely gone.

When I was sure it was safe to move, I walked over to Mr. Johnson's door, wondering if he'd locked it as he left. But when I turned the handle, it unlatched and the door opened into his office.

The next few moments happened so fast!

I looked around for anything different from the last time I was there.

I saw a box marked Junk in the
corner. Bingo!

I opened the box. It was full of Bonus Bucks and rewards. Pushing aside all the stuff I didn't need, I looked for the one badge I had come for. Sitting at the very bottom of the box, there it was!

Now it was time for phase three! The most awesome and dangerous phase of all.

# CHAPTER 19

**E**arlier today, in the middle of Ms. Gaffey's afternoon reading time, I had decided that for phase three of my plan, after I grabbed the badge, I would run out the recess doors.

So, now that I had the badge in my back pocket, I ran across the playground and around to the front of the school. I stopped when I got to the corner to make sure that none of the parents or guardians or Mr. Johnson was outside.

When I knew that the coast was clear, I took off running down the street. I'd never run so fast in my whole life.

*Reminder to self: Next time I make a plan like this, there has to be less running.*

When I saw the big white house with the gray door and the fence around back, I knew I had made it! I walked around to the back and opened the wooden fence door.

Mary Ann sat on the edge of her deck in a bright pink bathing suit. It had a frilly fluff around the middle and looked just like her ballet outfit. She was looking at her feet like they had turned into onions. Mary Ann hated onions!

Jenny sat next to her. "You and I will still have fun," she said. "Really!"

I cleared my throat.

Mary Ann looked up.

"You!" she said.

At first I thought she said "you" like "Yay! You're here! My old best friend!"

But then I realized she said "you" like "Oh no! Yuck! What's my ex-best friend doing here?"

Normally, I'd throw my hood up and get all kinds of angry if someone said that to me. But instead I just stared at my feet and felt myself get warm.

"Nobody's here because of that big fight you were in at recess," she yelled. "They all got in trouble and had to go home."

"Yeah, well," I started to say, "that's cuz I was trying to . . . ," but then I stopped talking.

I wanted to tell her that the whole thing was for her. But she was so mad that I didn't feel like it would make any difference.

"Never mind. It doesn't matter," I said. "I can't stay either. I just wanted to give you your gift."

I pulled the badge out of my pocket and stuck my hand out. Mary Ann looked at it.

"How . . . how did you get that?" she said.

"I shouldn't tell you," I said. "But there's no way Mr. Johnson will convince Principal Roberta to get rid of the bucks altogether. I just don't believe that. So you should be able to use it eventually."

Mary Ann took the badge from my hand.

"Thanks," she said so quietly I almost didn't hear her.

I turned around to leave. I didn't have a lot of time to get back.

"Wait!"

I spun back around.

"Why didn't you tell me you weren't coming to my ballet recital?" Mary Ann asked.

"My dad called your mom but—"

"Wait, what?"

I took a few steps closer. "My mom had to work last minute, and you know my dad can't drive. He called your mom and asked her to call him back, but he never heard anything."

Mary Ann's face turned back to the stinky onion face.

"I know!" I said a little too loud. "I know! I miss out on all kinds of stuff because of them, but I tried to see if I could go with you. I am really, really sorry, Mary Ann. Really! I wanted to be there!"

And then her mad face melted away. "My mom lost her phone that morning and had to get a new one. She never got the message," she said.

It was quiet for a few seconds. Then Jenny smiled and waved me toward her. "You should stay. Right, Mary Ann?"

I felt like my heart had my hand wrapped around it. While I waited for Mary Ann to answer, my chest felt tight, and it made my lungs tight, and I couldn't breathe.

Mary Ann nodded. She smiled and looked at me like I was a piece of chocolate cake, and Mary Ann loves *everything* chocolate!

"Yeah," Mary Ann said. "Please stay."

All the air came back to my lungs, and my heart stretched itself out. I knew I was supposed to run back to the school. I knew if I didn't,

Mr. Johnson would definitely be able to tell I wasn't in the bathroom. I knew I'd get in-school suspension.

But in that moment, I didn't care.

"Okay," I said. "But just for one game."

When I looked up and saw the sun going down, my whole body felt tight.

"Oh no! I have to go!" I yelled.

I ran up the street, across the playground, back into the school, and down the hallways. My legs felt like wet spaghetti as I stood in the middle of the cafeteria.

*Reminder to self again: Next time, make a plan with ZERO running.*

*Second reminder to self: Ask Dad if he'll make spaghetti for dinner sometime soon.*

"Where did everybody go?" I said to nobody.

But somebody heard it.

"Well . . . well . . . well . . ."

I turned around and knew exactly who it was.

"I knew you'd show your face eventually," said Mr. Johnson. "You're serving in-school suspension starting Monday morning! Your parents and the police are in my office. Let's head there, shall we?"

I walked along with Mr. Johnson. Getting ISS was the worst news of my life.

But I still had to smile.

# CHAPTER 20

**MONDAY, OCTOBER 10**

**W**hen you have in-school suspension, you have to show up to school at the same time as everyone else, so the bus ride to school this morning was weird. While everybody acted like it was a normal day, I knew mine wouldn't be normal at all.

My head hung as low as it would go without falling off. That is, until I walked into the principal's office.

*What is going on?* I thought.

"You, my dear Robin, have some very good friends," said Principal Roberta.

"That's . . . great," I said. "Where should I go for my suspension?"

Then I was even more surprised.

That's when Mary Ann raised her hand. "Actually," she said, and pointed to her Principal for the Day badge pinned to the front of her T-shirt, "I have something to say about that."

"We all do," Sammy said.

"When I woke up on Saturday morning," LJ said, "I called Mary Ann."

I looked at Mary Ann, but she was looking at LJ.

LJ went on, "I told Mary Ann all about what you'd done this week, and how mean Nadia had been to you, and how I had to stand up for you. And that's why I didn't make it to her birthday party."

"But what she didn't know," Mary Ann said, "was that Sammy had also just called me to tell me the same thing. And Allana and Dale called me a little while later."

"So we all agreed to come in here and tell Principal Roberta about what happened."

I felt my cheeks get warm. I put my hood up and pulled on the strings, but Mary Ann grabbed my hand.

"You were so brave," she whispered.

Then I felt my cheeks get so hot, I thought someone had sneaked the whole school into an oven when I wasn't looking.

I thought Mr. Johnson would tell me to put my hood back down, but he just stood there and stared across the room at the wall, his arms across his chest.

But I still didn't know why they were all in the principal's office now.

"So . . . ," I said.

"So," Sammy said, "you don't have suspension! Come on, Robin! Pick up the clues!"

Dale and Allana rapped back and forth:

*It wasn't just your fault*
*It was Nadia's, too*
*It was really all her fault*

*Well, maybe a little bit you*
   *But we all agreed*
*To tell your story*
   *And Principal Roberta*
*Is at least forty!*

Everybody looked at Allana. Her face had turned as red as a ripe strawberry! "Principal Roberta, I'm so sorry. 'Story' was hard to rhyme with . . ." She looked at Dale. "You were right! Being the one to rhyme all the time is really hard!"

"How about I step in now?" Principal Roberta said. Allana nodded her head and backed up behind Dale.

"Mary Ann came to me this morning and asked if she could use her Principal for the Day badge today. Since it was my first day back from the conference, frankly, I was relieved! Then she asked if her first duty as Principal for the Day could be to reverse your in-school suspension.

"As you can imagine, I was surprised to hear any student had received in-school suspension in the very short time I was gone. Especially a student with no previous record.

"Before I could walk to Mr. Johnson's office to ask him

about it, the rest of your friends arrived. They explained to me what they'd explained to Mary Ann. I called Mr. Johnson in to ask him to confirm what they'd told me. He had a different opinion about the cause of the events, but the events themselves were the same." She looked at Mr. Johnson. Everyone did then. He just kept staring at the wall. He tightened his arms across his chest.

Principal Roberta turned back to me. "I can understand why you'd get very upset, given everything that happened. I'd like to talk to you during recess today," Principal

Roberta said, "about your... actions and how sometimes they go sideways from what you intend. Maybe we can find a way to ensure you don't have any more injured classmates when stressful events happen."

"Okay," I said. "Thanks."

Principal Roberta clapped her hands together. "Very well. Then I would like for you all to return to class."

In a mad rush, all of my friends ran toward me and hugged me in one big squeeze. It was both really great and a little too much.

As we walked out of the office, I heard Principal Roberta say,

"Well, Mary Ann, as Principal for the Day, what would you like to do next?"

"I'd like to call Nadia to our office to question her about shaking down kids for Bonus Bucks and for being a mean, mean kid and a bully and a bad nickname giver! I think you should play the good cop, and I'll play the bad cop."

Principal Roberta pinched the area between her eyes. "How about we allow Nadia to tell her side of the story, and we'll take it from there."

"Okay," Mary Ann said, "but first I'd like to make an announcement."

There was a *tap-tap-tap* on the speakers. We all stayed right outside the principal's office to listen. Mary Ann's voice boomed. "Attention Nottingham Elementary. As Principal for the Day, I'm happy to report that the Bonus Bucks system will resume beginning immediately. That is all."

I turned around to see Mr. Johnson's face. He rolled his eyes and shook his head as he walked back to his office.

Then Mary Ann ran out of Principal Roberta's office and stopped right in front of me.

"Hey," she said, "do you think Jenny and I could sit with all of you at lunch?"

"I don't know," I said. "We're a pretty picky group."

Mary Ann looked at me like I'd turned into a bowl of French onion soup!

I laughed. "Duh. You guys can definitely sit with us."

Mary Ann smiled. "Good!" she said, and went back into Principal Roberta's office.

We all headed back to Ms. Gaffey's classroom.

"I wish she hadn't brought up lunch," LJ said. "I'm starving."

"Me, too!" I said. "Maybe I'll just eat my chicken, apple, and cheddar cheese sandwich before class starts."

LJ looked at me like I was crazy.

"Hey, I'm an outlaw now," I said. "Lunch is anytime I want it to be."

Allana and Dale burst out laughing as we all walked into our classroom, ready for our math lesson.

And lunch. I was so so so ready for lunch.

# THE END

# DIARY OF A 5TH GRADE
# OUTLAW
## THE FRIEND THIEF

## SATURDAY, OCTOBER 15

"Hey," Mary Ann whispered. "Would you like to come over for dinner?"

My smile grew to the size of a birthday cake. Mary Ann hadn't invited me over to her house since we'd become friends again.

I looked back at LJ, Sammy, Allana, and Dale. They were all standing in a circle on the basketball court.

I felt a little bad leaving them before the game was over, but I had spent *all* day with them. I was pretty sure they wouldn't mind if I went to Mary Ann's.

I nodded to Mary Ann and her smile was as big as a watermelon.

Then Mary Ann ran over to her mom.

I decided to tell my friends I was leaving. I told them as fast as I could. Like, all the words were actually parts of one big word.

"Hey-guys-Mary-Ann-invited-me-to-dinner-and-I-said-yes-so-I'm-going-to-go-this-was-fun-I'll-see-you-guys-at-school-on-Monday."

At first they all blinked and stared at me like my face was covered in pink frosting and they weren't sure if it was strawberry or watermelon flavored.

But then Sammy, Allana, and Dale all came over and high-fived me.

And then a weird thing happened. I stood there, waiting to say "see ya later" to LJ, but she didn't say goodbye to me. She didn't even look at me. Instead, LJ knelt down and tried to get something off the bottom of her shoe.

I didn't know what to do, so I waved to everybody else, ran over to the car, and got in the back seat next to Mary Ann. As we drove away, I looked through the window back at my friends. They were all playing ball, except LJ. She was looking at me like she still couldn't tell what flavor that frosting was on my face.

My stomach sank into my feet. What was going on with LJ?

## ABOUT THE AUTHOR

Gina Loveless lives in eastern Pennsylvania with her husband, son, and two dogs. She fell in love with kids' books when she was eight and fell back in love with them when she was twenty-eight. Her humorous health and wellness book, *Puberty Is Gross, but Also Really Awesome*, will be published in 2020.

## ABOUT THE ILLUSTRATOR

Andrea Bell is an illustrator and comic artist living in Chicago through the best and worst seasons. She enjoys rock climbing, making playlists, being surrounded by nature, and indulging in video games.

# DIARY OF A 5TH GRADE OUTLAW

Andrews McMeel Publishing
a division of Andrews McMeel Universal
1130 Walnut Street, Kansas City, Missouri 64106

www.andrewsmcmeel.com

Epic! Creations, Inc.
702 Marshall Street, Suite 280, Redwood, California 94063

www.getepic.com

19 20 21 22 23 SHD 10 9 8 7 6 5 4 3 2 1

Paperback ISBN: 978-1-5248-5526-0
Hardback ISBN: 978-1-5248-5548-2

Library of Congress Control Number: 2019905308

Design by Dan Nordskog

Made by:
Sheridan Books, Inc.
Address and location of manufacturer:
613 E. Industrial Drive
Chelsea, Michigan 48118
1st Printing—8/2/19